The lump of gold rests heavy on Hans' back.

A passing gentleman is kind enough to offer an exchange.
For surely, a trusty steed would serve Hans better than the gold?

MISS OUT   UPGRADE   MISS OUT   UPGRADE

Seven years of toil drag by.

At long last, wages in return for work.

Alas! Hans is promptly unhorsed.

Praise luck, a virtuous farmer comes to his aid.

ANON

Stuff making you sick?
Give this a whirl.

GET A BEER BELLY

PEDAL FORWARD

A placid cow in return for the wild horse? A fine trade! Hans counts himself lucky.

The farmer rides away on his new fortune, while Hans trudges on.

With a glad heart, Hans hurries homewards with his goose.

Elsewhere, the considerate men who have lightened Hans' burden appear to be doing well.

GAMEMASTER

You're late! Quick, take this. Spend it, your choices are unlimited.

WELCOME HAN5

TURN BACK

ACCEPT ORB

As for Hans, a friendly miller stops him. Of what use is a goose? A grindstone lasts much longer.

Egad! The leaden grindstone slips away with a splash.

If a classic is a tale that outlives its time, what form could Hans' story take today? A successful life, in contemporary terms, is about maximising individual happiness—largely through the pleasures of consumption. And yet there is an irony in the uncertainty and anxiety that invariably surrounds the experience. Most people are insecure, constantly looking for advice and reassurance.

A contemporary Hans might well struggle with shopping for the best bargains, looking for the optimal choice amongst the dizzying and seemingly limitless options that promise happiness. He is likely to be bewildered by the 'commodity fetishism', which sets up its own spiral of exchange, leaving him burdened with things he has no use for. A situation where the value of objects is connected more to covetousness than to actual use is truly surreal.

Here is one way of exploring the choices that Hans is called on to make, set within the framework of consumer capitalism. This interpretation of the story draws from the 'Choose Your Adventure' genre and the aesthetics of a video game. Hans is seemingly handed control of his choices, story and destiny. Invoking a sense of both bottoms-up agency and top-down control, he is given opportunities to choose. But ironically, the available options and their possible outcomes appear to be decided already. How are choices rewarded and discouraged? Is a choice truly free within a framework of possibilities and parameters? Should not a fuller notion of freedom include the choice not to participate at all? The pleasure of navigating this form of narrative is not necessarily in finding the singular 'best' ending, but in flipping back and forth through all the choices, experiences and endings that are offered.

It could well turn out that what Hans really wants is a return to the human values that were lost along the way: happiness, freedom and mutual care.

But... no matter. Hans is equal to this twist of fate. Light of weight and happy of heart, he knocks on his mother's door. Free at last!